'Be kind. When kindness becomes part of something it beautifies it,
and when it is removed from something it spoils it.'
– Prophet Mohammed (peace be upon him),
who taught me what kindness means.

This book is for all the precious little souls devastated by war.
For Usman, best-friend-husband/bookshop-buddy/believer-in-me.
For Mum, teacher-of-wonder/book-hoarder.
For Dad, bedtime-story-inventor/library-tripper.
Hi Hamza! Favourite sibling.
– H.N.K

For Maman and Dad
– L.C

Macmillan Children's Books have made a donation
to a charity that helps people in conflict.

First published 2020 by Macmillan Children's Books
an imprint of Pan Macmillan
The Smithson, 6 Briset Street, London EC1M 5NR
Associated companies throughout the world
www.panmacmillan.com

ISBN: 978-1-5290-3213-0

1 3 5 7 9 8 6 4 2

A CIP catalogue record for this book is available from the British Library.

Printed in China

WRITTEN BY
HIBA NOOR KHAN

ILLUSTRATED BY
LAURA CHAMBERLAIN

THE Little War Cat

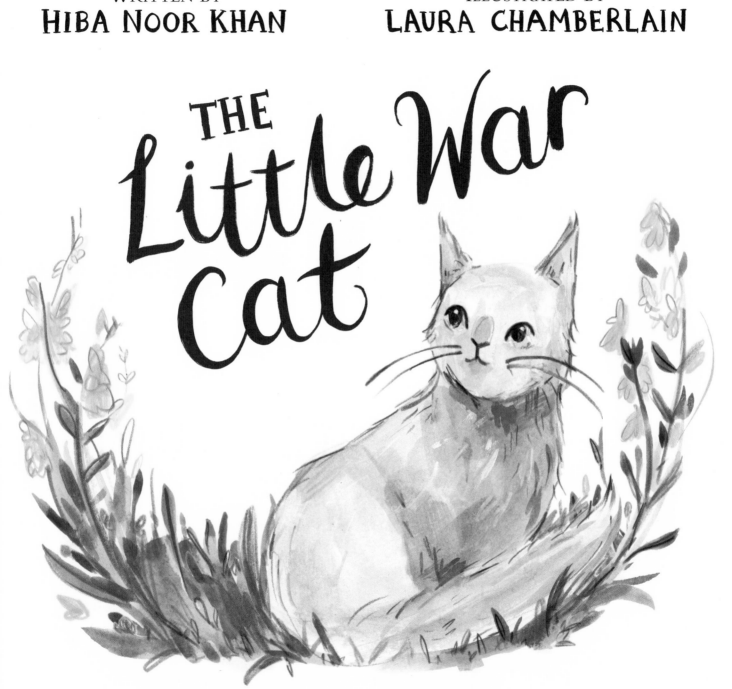

MACMILLAN CHILDREN'S BOOKS

There was once a little grey cat who lived in Aleppo.
She would play tag in the marble mosques,
and sunbathe beneath the palm trees.

But when the humans
in boots came, the sun
seemed to disappear . . .

and everything changed.

One dark day, the little cat was feeling lonely and hungry.
She wandered the streets she knew like the back of her paw.

Past where the butcher's shop used to be,
the baker's, the cheesemaker's.

But after a full day of sniffing and searching,
she didn't see any of her friends, and there was no food to be found.

By the time the stars rose,
she hung her little head
and wished life was like it was before.

Suddenly, there was a
BANG and a CRASH!
It was the humans again,
with their big noisy boots.

The little grey cat felt frozen to the spot, her whiskers trembling.

Days and nights passed,
but the cat stayed in the
shadows, hungry and scared.

Until one day, she noticed a different human.

This one didn't make bangs and crashes.

This human had a gentle voice and spoke kind words.

The little grey cat followed the human.
She wove through the streets of Aleppo,
past empty houses and broken furniture.

Just as she
thought her
paws could
go no further,

they came to a quiet spot.
She could not believe her eyes.

Friends! Food! And no big noisy boots.

She wanted to join them,
but she still felt scared.
She remembered the
bangs and the crashes.

The kind human spotted her hiding in the corner.

He brought her fish to eat,
and stayed with her all night long.

By sunrise, the little grey cat was feeling like herself again.

She played tag, and ate so much fish she had to flop down in the sun.

She thanked the
gentle human for
leading her to a
kinder place.

Then, from the corner of her eye,
the little grey cat saw something.

Under a table, a
trembling shadow,

a small
blue
shoe.

It was a little boy, frozen to the spot.
The cat knew exactly what to do.

She wound herself around
the little boy's legs,

and purred her loudest.

Then she brought
the boy bread and
curled up on his lap,

warming his cold hands.

And slowly, slowly but surely,
the magic that worked on the little grey cat . . .

worked on the little boy too.

A note from Hiba

I was inspired to write this story
by Mohammad Alaa Aljaleel, from Syria.
When war came to his city, he began
driving ambulances to help the injured people.
Even when his family left for safety, he stayed and set
up a sanctuary, which became home to hundreds of cats.
This is how he got the nickname, 'The Cat Man of Aleppo'.
Adults and children came to the sanctuary to help and play,
making it a place of love and hope for everyone.

This story is for the millions of children and animals
affected by wars, every year, all over the world.
After working to help war victims and visiting
refugee camps, I saw for myself how homes and loved
ones are lost, but hope never is. A little kindness goes a long
way. As we can see from the story, there is a ripple effect,
spreading to many people, animals and places.

Can you think of ways you can be kind? It could be
as simple as saying something nice, lending a
helping hand or even just smiling at someone!

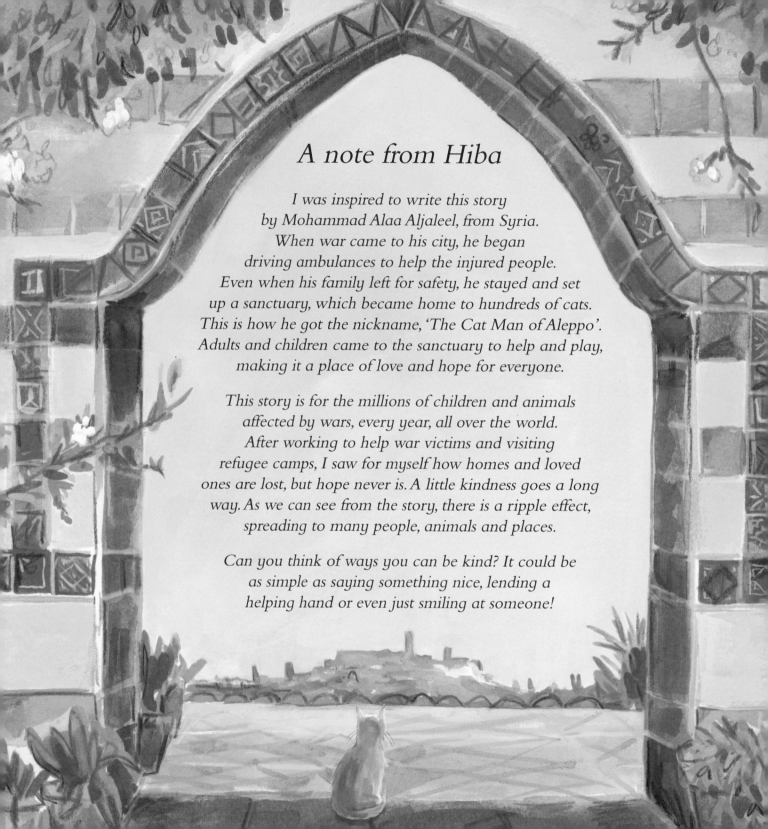